KU-285-281

To Lucy

From. Luce

Written by Katherine Sully
Illustrated by Julia Seal
Designed by Nicola Moore

First published by HOMETOWN WORLD in 2017
Hometown World Ltd
7 Northumberland Buildings
Bath
BA1 2JB

www.hometownworld.co.uk

Follow us @hometownworldbooks

LUCY
Santa's Secret
Elf

Hometown World

It was Christmas Eve and Lucy
was tucked up in bed at home.
She was trying so hard to be asleep.
But she could hear strange noises.

It wasn't the sound of sleigh bells.
It wasn't the sound of reindeer hoofs on the roof.
It wasn't even the sound of Santa unpacking his sack.

It was more of a

HARUMPH!

and an

OOF!

It was no good.

There'd be no sleep for Lucy
until she'd found out what
was making that noise.

Lucy crept down the stairs
and peered into the living room.
There were three stockings
hanging from the chimney.

One of them belonged to Lucy.
But where did the other two come from?
Suddenly, a muffled voice came from the chimney.

"Oh dear.
I'm even
more
stuck now!"

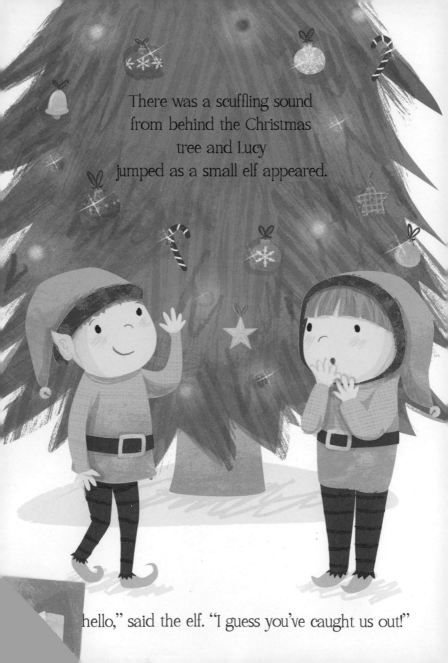

There was a scuffling sound
from behind the Christmas
tree and Lucy
jumped as a small elf appeared.

hello," said the elf. "I guess you've caught us out!"

Lucy listened as the elf explained
how Santa was stuck in the chimney.
The elf had tried to pull him out. But the only
things that had come down so far were
Santa's boots and trousers!

"I can help you," suggested Lucy.
"I'll hold Santa's feet and we can both pull."
The elf agreed. "Between us, we might be
able to get him unstuck."

Lucy grasped both of Santa's feet firmly.
But, just at that moment, a light went on upstairs.
"Lucy, is that you?" called her mum.
"Back to bed now, please, or Santa won't come!"

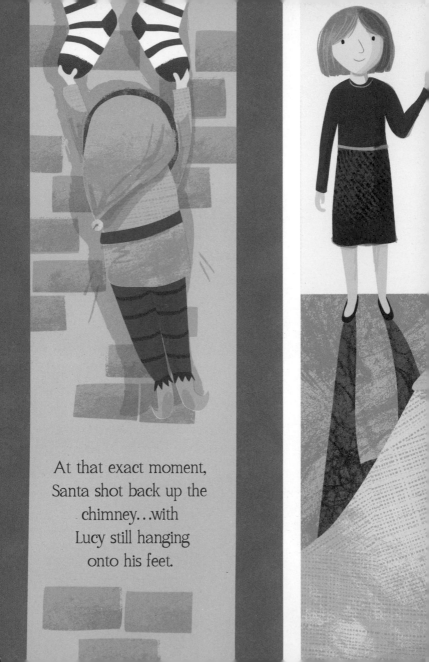

At that exact moment,
Santa shot back up the
chimney...with
Lucy still hanging
onto his feet.

The poor elf could not believe his eyes.
But there was no time to think…
Lucy's mum was coming
out of her bedroom.

"Just coming!" squeaked the elf.
The elf hurried up the stairs and jumped into Lucy's
bed, pulling the covers up over his head.
"Night-night, sweetie!" said Lucy's
mum through the doorway.

Meanwhile, up on the roof, Santa and Lucy
had landed in a heap. The clever reindeer had
hooked their reins under Santa's arms and
pulled as hard as they could.

"Well done, chaps!" said Santa brushing
himself down. "No more mince pies for
me tonight!"

Lucy scrambled to her feet. But Santa was so busy, he didn't notice that Lucy and the elf had swapped places!

"I think we'd better deliver the rest of the presents first," said Santa, "and leave this house till last."

Santa climbed into the driving seat.

"Elf, you get the parcels ready for our next destination," he called over his shoulder. "But I'm not Elf..." replied Lucy.

Santa wasn't really listening.
He was talking to the reindeer.
"Up, up and away!" Santa called and
the reindeer took off before Lucy
had time to explain.

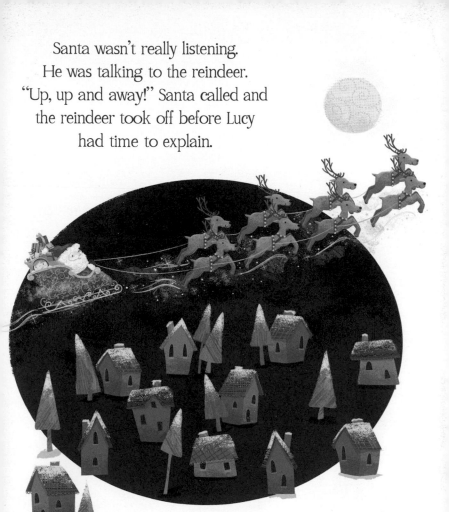

Lucy clung on tight as the
sleigh climbed high into the
night sky above the rooftops.

Surrounded by parcels, Lucy
was so busy working out which sacks were
which, there was no time to let Santa
know that there'd been a mistake.

There were **big** parcels for the cities,

and **SHINY** parcels for the towns.

There were **ODD**-shaped parcels for the villages,

and **mystery** parcels for the farms.

To: Lucy

As they landed at their next stop,
Santa decided that he couldn't risk
getting stuck in a chimney again.

"Elf, I think you'd better make the deliveries
from now on," decided Santa,
"while I sort out the parcels."

Lucy *shimmied* down chimneys.

She **squeezed** through cat flaps.

And, if all else failed, she used Santa's *magic* key to let herself in.

In each house, Lucy collected the mince pies to take home to Mrs Santa, and carrots for the reindeer.

Finally, there was just one sack left, and
Santa still hadn't realised his mistake!
The sleigh headed back over the
rooftops to Lucy's house.

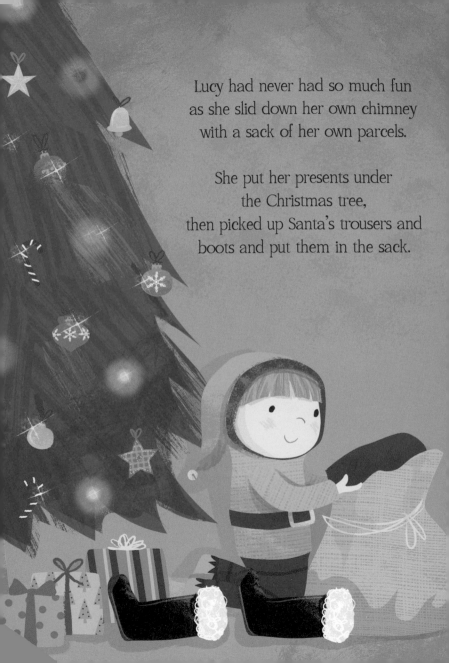

Lucy had never had so much fun
as she slid down her own chimney
with a sack of her own parcels.

She put her presents under
the Christmas tree,
then picked up Santa's trousers and
boots and put them in the sack.

"Psst! Elf, where are you?" whispered Lucy.

A very happy Elf appeared rubbing his eyes.
"I've had such a lovely sleep," he said.
Lucy handed over the sack and
waved as Elf disappeared
up the chimney.

Back in her cosy bed, Lucy
listened to the sound of reindeer hoofs
on the roof, sleigh bells and, very faintly,

"Ho ho ho!
Merry Christmas!"

Or was that,

"Ho ho ho!
yummy mince pies!"?

Write your name on the parcel labels.